GUMPA AND THE PAINT BOX

First published by Collins in 1949.
Published in Great Britain, 1997, by
Pookie Productions Ltd
12 Craighouse Avenue
Edinburgh EH10 5LN

British Library Cataloguing-in-Publication Data
A Catalogue record of this book is available
from the British Library.

ISBN 1 872885 50 0

Designed and typeset in 16/20pt Stone Informal
by Janet Watson

Reproduction by Mitchell Graphics, Glasgow

Printed by Craft Print Pte Ltd

The Animal Shelf

GUMPA AND THE PAINT BOX

Written and Illustrated by
Ivy Wallace

POOKIE PRODUCTIONS
Beautiful Books for Children

The Animals on their Shelf

GUMPA AND THE PAINT BOX

Early one morning, Timothy's Special Animals were all fast asleep on their Shelf in his bedroom.

Then Stripey the zebra woke up, stretched and yawned. He was careful not to wake Getup the giraffe or Gumpa the bear.

Stripey wondered if Woeful was awake, but the little monkey's face was tucked under his paws.

"Are you awake, Little Mut?" whispered Stripey.

"No, I'm still asleep," replied Little Mut, snuggling into a tight ball.

Stripey looked down at Timothy's bed but he was asleep too.

Suddenly Gumpa the bear opened his eyes and said, "Mood Gorning!"

"I beg your pardon?" said Stripey politely.

"Mood Gorning!" repeated Gumpa.

"Are you all right, Gumpa?" asked Stripey anxiously.

Gumpa shook his head, " Wromething is song mith we!"

Stripey woke the others. "Something is wrong with Gumpa!"

"I'm frack to bont," explained Gumpa whose head had turned back to front in the night. "I nall *shever* palk troperly again!"

"Of course you'll talk properly again, Gumpa," said Timothy who had been woken by the noise. "Don't talk rubbish!"

"I'm not ralking tubbish!" cried Gumpa angrily. "Co-one nares about me!"

"Of course we care about you, Gumpa," comforted the other animals. "Don't be silly!"

"I'm not seeing billy!" snapped Gumpa, stamping his paw on Woeful's tail. He stumped to the end of the Shelf and turned his front on them all.

"Now he's going to sulk all morning," said Woeful, tenderly stroking his trodden-on tail.

"I'm *not* soing to gulk," muttered Gumpa in a sad voice. "I am ery, ery vill. I deed a noctor."

(Really, the naughty little bear knew perfectly well that he only had to turn his head round to be all right again!)

Timothy (who guessed Gumpa was just pretending) dressed quickly and ran off to breakfast.

Gumpa lay on the Shelf on his tummy with his eyes closed. "Moor pe," he murmured faintly, "Goor Pumpa!"

"Have you a pain?" asked Stripey.

"Pundreds of hains!" groaned Gumpa.

"Where are they?" asked Getup.

"In ty mummy," sighed Gumpa, rubbing his back where his tummy should have been.

"Poor Gumpa won't want any breakfast," said Timothy, putting a plate up on the Shelf.

Gumpa opened one eye. "I lould wike a little," he murmured. "Just tuttered boast and a mittle larmalade, please."

Timothy shook his head firmly. "I'm the doctor," he reminded Gumpa. "No food!"

Gumpa groaned louder than ever.

The other Animals enjoyed their toast and marmalade. They finished every crumb and licked their paws well.

Timothy borrowed a doll's bed from Judy who lives next door.
Gumpa lay on his tummy with his face looking upwards.

"Do you feel any better?" squeaked Little Mut.

Gumpa shook his head sadly. "I am pery voorly,"
he whispered. "I need thood gings to eat . . . lots of thood gings!"

"You must have some medicine," decided Timothy, busy with some orange juice.

"*Mo nedicine!*" squealed Gumpa. "I swon't wallow it !"

"You will swallow it !" said Timothy, holding the little bear's head firmly. Gumpa had to swallow it. Then he dived under the covers, angry and spluttering.

"Now you must rest, Gumpa," said Timothy. "I'm taking the other Animals to the sweet shop. It is a pity you're poorly!"

And away went Timothy with the others.

Gumpa was furious. He rolled on to his back and turned his head round the proper way.

"I thought they'd make a fuss of me," he muttered, "and give me good things to eat."

Then the little bear saw Timothy's paintbox . . .

"I'll paint myself all over with red spots!" decided the naughty little bear. "Timothy knew I was just pretending before. Now I'll be able to stay in bed and have heaps of good things to eat!"

When Timothy and the others came back, they crowded round Gumpa's bed.

"Look at Gumpa!" cried Timothy. "He's covered with red spots! I think he's got measles!"

"Poor Gumpa!" whispered the others.

"Keep away or you may catch them!" warned Timothy. "I'd better move Gumpa away from you all."

Timothy put Gumpa's bed up on the chest of drawers. "I'm so sorry, little fellow," he whispered. "I know you were pretending before but I can see you're ill this time."

Stripey and Getup trotted off to get trays of food ready. Woeful and Little Mut brought him bunches of flowers.

All day Gumpa pretended to be ill. He had trays of lovely food to eat and presents of flowers.

After tea he said, "Thank you all for being so kind. I'm better now!"

"You can't be!" said Timothy. "You still have your spots. Measles takes a long time. You must stay in bed until your spots go."

So night-time found the silly little bear still alone on the chest of drawers.

Next morning Gumpa's spots had vanished! (They had taken him a long time to lick off in the night!)

"I'm better!" he called across to the Animal Shelf.

But no-one listened to him . . . they were far too busy looking at Little Mut! He was covered with pink spots from the tips of his ears to the tip of his tail!

"I've measled in the night!" he squeaked. "Now I can be with Gumpa!"

Timothy borrowed another bed from Judy. Little Mut sat in it surrounded by comfy pillows and trays of good things to eat and flowers. He smiled happily across to Gumpa.

"I did it so I could keep you company," he whispered.

But Gumpa didn't smile back. He stared at Little Mut's spots and frowned and frowned.

At last it was night time. When the other Animals were asleep on their Shelf, Gumpa whispered to Little Mut, "You'd better start licking those spots off! Then we can get up tomorrow. I'm tired of being in bed!"

So Little Mut started licking. In the darkness his tiny tongue made a *lish-lish* noise. For a long time he licked and licked until the noise became *lisher-lisher-lisher.*

But it was no use. *The spots would not move!*

"Gumpa, they won't lick off!" he whispered.

"They *must* or we'll have to stay in bed for ever," whispered Gumpa angrily. "Lick harder!"

Lisher-lisher-lisher-lisher went Little Mut until his tongue ached. "It's no use!" he whispered. "They won't lick off!"

"But paint should lick off," said Gumpa.

"It's not paint!" said Little Mut. "It's red stuff out of a bottle on Timothy's desk!"

"You silly Little Mut!" squealed Gumpa so loudly that
Timothy switched on the light.

"He's measled himself with your red ink!" cried Gumpa.
"It will *never* come off!"

Little Mut covered his face with his paws and sobbed.
"I will be spotted forever!"

"We'll get you right in the morning," comforted Timothy.

Next morning they put Little Mut in a bowl of hot, soapy water.

All the Animals helped to scrub him. Then they took him out, rinsed him and dried him. But the spots were still there!

"I'll have to go to school now," said Timothy and away he went.

Suddenly Getup had an idea. "My spots came off when we played Robinson Crusoe and I fell into Splashing Stream!"

"Maybe there's something special about stream water!" cried Stripey. "Let's try that!"

They all hurried downstairs and out into the garden.

When they reached Splashing Stream Woeful said, "We'll tie a string round his paw for safety and walk him along the edge in the shallow water."

They took turns in walking him up and down the edge of the stream. But when he came out his spots were pinker and brighter than ever.

"We *could* dip him in red ink and make a pink-all-over Little Mut," suggested Getup. But the others didn't like the idea.

When Timothy came home from school he said, "Your troubles are nearly over, Little Mut! I asked how to get ink spots off white wool and the answer is some stuff called ink remover! It's expensive but mum will get some for us, if we help her with some chores. First, we'll shell these peas."

The Animals set to work.

Then they weeded the garden path.

All the long afternoon the Shelf Animals worked. Getup and Stripey pulled out weeds and Woeful collected them into heaps.

Gumpa told everybody what to do and Little Mut had rides in the wheelbarrow to the compost heap and back.

Then Timothy's mother gave them her sewing basket to tidy.

The Animals set to work until bedtime. Little Mut sorted buttons, Stripey and Getup tidied wools, Woeful wound cotton reels and Gumpa sat on the lid and told everybody what to do.

Next day, Timothy's mother bought a bottle of ink remover. They all helped dab it on Little Mut with pieces of cotton wool.

One by one the spots disappeared!

When they had all gone, Little Mut thanked everybody. "Id wad very kide ob you," he said. "Atishoo! I thig I hab caught a code id my nose through being washed so buch yesterday!"

Getup and Stripey galloped to Judy's home and brought back the little bed. Everybody helped tuck Little Mut in cosily. They brought him a hot water bottle, bunches of flowers and nice things to eat. But Little Mut was really ill this time.

He said, "Dow, thag you" in a faint squeak to the things to eat and lay all day with his eyes closed.

Gumpa felt awful. "It's all my fault he's boorly . . . I mean poorly," he said. "I will never pretend to be ill again!"

Next day Little Mut was much better. He sat wrapped in a warm shawl and Gumpa looked after him all day.

"It was all my fault, Little Mut," he said. "I pretended to be ill just to get good things to eat. But you pretended so you could keep me company. You are a much nicer Animal than I am!"

Next day Little Mut was quite better and Timothy took the Animals down to Foxglove Wood.

"Grass would look funny pink instead of green," said Gumpa wisely.

"Buttercups would look funny pink too!" agreed Woeful.

"A blue apple would look strange," decided Getup.

"A blue carrot would too!" agreed Stripey.

"A Little Mut should be white with a pink bow!" said Timothy.

And all the Animals agreed, as they looked proudly at their dear Little Mut, snow-white and smiling in the sunshine.